Dear Parent:

Buckle up! You are about to join your child on a very exciting journey. The destination? Independent reading!

Road to Reading will help you and your child get there. The program offers books at five levels, or Miles, that accompany children from their first attempts at reading to successfully reading on their own. Each Mile is paved with engaging stories and delightful artwork.

Getting Started
For children who know the alphabet and are eager to begin reading
• easy words • fun rhythms • big type • picture clues

Reading With Help
For children who recognize some words and sound out others with help
• short sentences • pattern stories • simple plotlines

Reading On Your Own
For children who are ready to read easy stories by themselves
• longer sentences • more complex plotlines • easy dialogue

First Chapter Books
For children who want to take the plunge into chapter books
• bite-size chapters • short paragraphs • full-color art

Chapter Books
For children who are comfortable reading independently
• longer chapters • occasional black-and-white illustrations

There's no need to hurry through the Miles. Road to Reading is designed without age or grade levels. Children can progress at their own speed, developing confidence and pride in their reading ability no matter what their age or grade.

So sit back and enjoy the ride—every Mile of the way!

For city cats Agatha,
Geisha, Cleo, Houdini,
and all their Otis country cousins

B.S.H.

To Sam

P.P.

Library of Congress Cataloging-in-Publication Data
Hazen, Barbara Shook.
City cats, country cats / by Barbara Shook Hazen ; illustrated by Pam Paparone.
    p.   cm. — (Road to reading.   Mile 1)
Summary: City cats and country cats engage in typical activities,
including riding bicycles, selling peanuts, driving tractors, and
feeding hens.
ISBN 0-307-26109-3 (pbk.) — ISBN 0-307-46109-2 (GB)
[1. Cats—Fiction.   2. City and town life—Fiction.   3. Country
life—Fiction.   4. Stories in rhyme.]   I. Paparone, Pam, ill.
II. Title.   III. Series.
PZ8.3.H339Ci   1999
[E]—dc21   98-37091
                                                              CIP
                                                              AC

A GOLDEN BOOK • New York
Golden Books Publishing Company, Inc. New York, New York 10106

ISBN: 0-307-26109-3 (pbk)
ISBN: 0-307-46109-2 (GB)

10   9   8   7   6   5   4   3   2

City Cats, Country Cats

by Barbara Shook Hazen
illustrated by Pam Paparone

City cats,

city cats.

Big cats,
small cats.

Short cats,
tall cats.

Gray cats,

white cats.

Black as night cats.

All of them

are city cats.

City cats
all like to play.

They like to play
in a city way.

City cats leap.
City cats creep.

City cats play
and go to sleep.

They sleep on mats.
They sleep in hats.

They sleep and dream
of city rats.

Country cats,

country cats.

Big cats,
small cats.

Short cats,
tall cats.

Gray cats,

white cats.

Black as night cats.

All of them

are country cats.

Country cats
all like to play.

They like to play
in a country way.

Country cats leap.
Country cats creep.

Country cats play
and go to sleep.

They sleep on mats.
They sleep in hats.

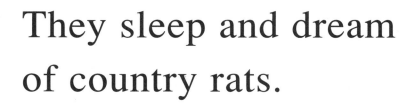

They sleep and dream
of country rats.

Good night, city cats.
Good night, country cats.

Good night, all cats!